Amish Weddings

The Widower's Baby

Book Two

Samantha Bayarr

This novel is a work of fiction. Names, characters, and incidents are the product of the author's imagination, and are therefore used fictitiously. Any similarity or resemblance to actual persons; living or dead, places or events is purely coincidental and beyond the intent of the author or publisher.

All brand names or product names mentioned in this book are the sole ownership of their respective holders. Livingston Hall Publishers is not associated with any products or brands named in this book

A note from the Author:

While this novel is set against the backdrop of an Amish community, the characters and the names of the community are fictional. There is no intended resemblance between the characters in this book or the setting, and any real members of any Amish or Mennonite community. As with any work of fiction, I've taken license in some areas of research as a means of creating the necessary circumstances for my characters and setting. It is completely impossible to be accurate in details and descriptions, since every community differs, and such a setting would destroy the fictional quality of entertainment this book serves to present. Any inaccuracies in the Amish and Mennonite lifestyles portrayed in this book are completely due to fictional license. Please keep in mind that this book is meant for fictional, entertainment purposes only, and is not written as a text book on the Amish.

Happy Reading

If you have not read Book ONE in this series, this book will not make much sense, as it is a continuing series that incorporates all the characters from each book. Click HERE to get a copy of Ellie's Homecoming.

Chapter 1

Lydia's tormented screams reached Eli all the way to the barn, filling him with a fear he'd never known before. Hannah had urged him to call for the doctor, explaining it was too much of a gamble for a midwife alone.

Was she as fearful as he was?

His beautiful wife had tried to insist she didn't need or want the doctor, but Eli had gone against her wishes, worry forcing a decision out of him.

Desperation motivated him as he dialed the number with a shaky hand. He'd had the phone installed in the barn for this exact kind of emergency, and he prayed now that the doctor would answer.

He paced impatiently on the floor of the barn, crushing the fresh hay beneath his feet, while he waited through four rings. When the voicemail began, he hung up, saying another hasty prayer asking for guidance.

Hannah had used the term *breech,* and he'd lost a foal recently for the same reason, and he was terrified of the same fate for his child.

Another chilling scream rent the air, startling him out of the stupor of his prayer. He focused on the phone and dialed the emergency line, begging for an ambulance with one long, ragged breath. Tears pooled in his eyes as he answered several questions that indicated the person on the other end of the line was just as afraid for the safety of his wife and child.

"Please hurry," Eli pleaded with the man. "I have to get back to *mei fraa.* She needs me."

He set the phone down, the man still trying to get him to answer, but Eli was not thinking straight. Stumbling back to the house, he pleaded with God to save his family, each heavy step bringing more anxiety as he made his way back to them.

Once inside, Lydia's screams made him cringe, but there was something different about them now. As he made his way up the stairs to their room, he realized they had become weak and faint.

Forcing his feet to take him to her bedside, he avoided the scene at the foot of the bed where Hannah mopped up blood from the sheets. The sight of it made his heart race, but he wouldn't let either of them know how terrified he was.

He collapsed onto his knees and buried his face in his wife's neck, kissing her and whispering in her ear.

"I'm here, Lydia. Be strong."

She let out another weak cry, and then he heard the squeal from his child. He looked back at the infant, feeling his wife's grip on his hand loosen.

He watched with unseeing eyes as Hannah placed the *boppli* in Lydia's waiting arms, her smile weak, but proud.

"She has your blue eyes," Lydia whispered to her husband. "And blond, curly hair like her *mamm.*"

Eli watched his wife coo to her new daughter, and look up into his eyes. Her eyes were cloudy and dull, and her face seemed weighted down with a sadness.

"I want *mei dochder* to have a *mamm,"* she said with great effort.

"She has a *mamm,* Lydia. She has you." He didn't like the labored sound of her voice, nor did he like the words she was speaking.

"Nee, I don't think I'm going to make it."

"Shh," he begged his wife, his lower lip quivering. "Please don't talk like that. I called an ambulance, and they're going to take you to the hospital, and everything is going to be just fine, ain't so, Hannah?"

He looked up at the young woman who was working desperately and frantically mopping up blood his wife was losing. She glanced at him only for a flicker of a moment, and then nodded as she focused her attention back to the emergency that his wife's condition presented.

Lydia kissed the baby's face and smiled.

"Name her Mira, after *mei mamm,"* she said, and then motioned weakly for Hannah to come nearer.

She reluctantly left her task, knowing it wasn't making much difference.

"Hannah," Lydia whispered. "I want you to be her *mamm."*

"Nee, you're her *mamm,* Lydia," she said, forcing a smile around the tears in her eyes.

"You're going to be chasing after her for many years to come."

She placed a hand on Lydia's arm, and then went back to the task of cleaning, but she knew if the ambulance didn't hurry, they were going to lose her.

Eli held her close, rocking her back and forth, willing her to live, but it was all in vain, and his heart sank at the reality. *"Gott,* please!" he whispered into her hair.

In the distance, he could hear the faint sound of sirens from the nearing ambulance.

Lydia smiled at her husband. "Promise me you'll marry Hannah so our *dochder* will have a *mamm."*

He hesitated, not wanting to commit to such a foolish thing.

"Promise me," she said weakly.

"I promise," he whispered, glancing briefly at Hannah, hoping she hadn't heard his promise, but she had.

Lydia exhaled weakly, and didn't draw another breath. He pulled her away from him and jostled her.

"*Gott,* please don't take her from me," he sobbed.

He could hear the ambulance pulling into the driveway of their home, but Eli knew it was too late. She'd already drawn her last breath, and there would not be another.

Chapter 2

Eli watched methodically as Hannah wept quietly while she prepared Lydia's body to be taken by the mortician, where she would be further prepared for burial, and then brought back for the funeral.

Nothing seemed real to him anymore.

His sister and *mamm* had gathered in the corner of the room quietly to watch the doctor check over his child.

He could hear her crying, but he couldn't go to her.

His *boppli.*

He hadn't even really looked at her, except when Lydia had pointed out the blond curls that matched her own.

It didn't matter now. The child belonged to Hannah. His wife had given her the child, and he would honor her wishes. He didn't know what to do with the child. He wasn't her *mamm,* and he had no idea how to be. A girl would need a woman's care more than she would need him, and he hadn't even been able to bring himself to looking at her a second time. He feared it would cause him to break down if he saw too much of his wife in the child.

Ellie stood next to her twin brother, trying to urge him away from the morbid scene in front of him. He held fast to Lydia's hand, staring blankly, but unmovable. She had to wonder if he even heard her or knew she was there. She prayed silently that her brother's mourning would not consume him.

It wasn't that she didn't feel he had a right to grieve, but he had a new daughter who would need him to be strong. She felt sorry for Hannah, who had confided in her about Lydia's last moment before she passed on, knowing what a burden such a promise could be. She tried to reassure Hannah that everything would be alright in a day or so. They would get through the funeral, but she agreed Eli would need some help with the *boppli.* Ellie had encouraged her to stay on for an extra week to help her brother with the transition. Not exactly knowing how to react to the dying wish of her sister-in-law, whom she barely knew, Ellie tried to assure Hannah that it would likely be forgotten in a few days.

Seeing her brother now, Ellie had to wonder if she believed that herself.

Eli's attention turned to Hannah as she cleaned the baby and wrapped her in a blanket. He could hear her soft breath as she presented the child to him. His arms would not reach out to her. He stared blankly at the bundle in front of him, but could not look at her face. Little gurgles and squeaks reverberated from the folds of the blankets, and the child seemed content where she was.

He shook his head, and put up a hand.

"*Nee,*" he said firmly, keeping his lower jaw clenched to keep it from quivering with sorrow. "She needs a *mamm.* You are her *mamm* now, Hannah."

Hannah's breath hitched. She pulled the infant close to her, feeling elation and sorrow swirling inside her. She'd overheard the promise Lydia had prompted from Eli, knowing he'd only accepted to appease his wife. Surely he didn't mean to give away his child. As much as she wanted to have a child of her own, she could not accept such a burden, for Eli would take her back when he was finished grieving, and she would mourn the child forever.

Ellie hadn't missed the look on Hannah's face, and it caused her to worry. She knew the deep desire her friend had for wanting a baby of her own, and it wasn't right for her brother to dangle that over her head, no matter how much he was grieving.

She placed a hand on her brother's shoulder. "You don't mean that," she whispered. "She needs you. You're her *familye.*"

"Nee," he said angrily. "*Mei familye* is gone. *Mei fraa* is dead, and the *boppli* is Hannah's. She will have to raise her alone, because I'm not marrying her the way I promised Lydia."

Tears pooled in his eyes, and he fled from the room, leaving Hannah holding his child.

Chapter 3

Eli rose from the edge of the bed, having ignored the desperate knocks at the door from his sister, knowing it was time for the funeral.

Nothing could prepare him for this, and even his prayers were too weak to comfort him. He'd slept for the past two days, not thinking about his child. He'd overheard his *mamm* and sister telling Hannah they would return with a couple of bottles so she could give the infant goat's milk. After he'd snatched a few things from the room he no longer shared with Lydia, he'd taken them out to the *dawdi haus,* where he'd remained for the past two days. He hadn't wanted to face what was before him, and now, as

Ellie knocked at the door relentlessly, he would have to.

His tongue stuck to the roof of his mouth as he tried to tell her to leave him alone, but she continued to knock and call out to him. His head ached as he stumbled to the door and opened it just a crack, his eyes squinting against the bright morning sun that streamed in through the opening.

Ellie stood there, clad in a black mourning dress and bonnet.

He couldn't look at her.

She stared at her brother's disheveled clothing that he'd likely slept in for the past two days, his auburn hair standing on end on one side. She felt sorry for him, and wanted to pull him into her arms and make the pain go away, but she couldn't imagine being in his place. She could see the torment in his blank stare, his posture speaking volumes of his pain.

"Hannah and *Mira* are waiting in the buggy with *Mamm* and Jonas. We'll wait for you to dress."

She'd spoken his child's name so softly; he'd barely heard her.

He didn't want to hear it; he simply nodded and closed the door.

His thoughts slammed against his brain; he didn't want to think anymore. He was a father; it was what he and Lydia had wanted so much, and now she was gone trying to give that to him. His arms were empty, and his heart was broken beyond repair. How could he go and bury his wife the way his family expected him to? He knew the community would frown if he was not there, and he also knew they would frown if the child was not there, but he couldn't deal with her right now. He had to get through the funeral and the meal afterward that he would be expected to attend.

He felt as if someone had knocked the wind out of him, and he hadn't the strength or the will to draw in a breath.

Had his *mamm* felt this way when she'd buried his *daed?*

One would never have known; she'd handled herself with grace and a quiet dignity. He couldn't do that; he wasn't as strong as she was.

He combed through his hair and looked at himself in the mirror, tugging on the long whiskers along his jaw. He'd grown the beard as an outward sign he was married, but now he was not.

He no longer had a wife.

I should have no beard, he thought to himself as he stared at his reflection.

Picking up a pair of scissors, he pulled a section of his beard and began to cut away at it angrily. His throat constricted as he remembered all the times Lydia would rake her fingers through it when they would cuddle. But as he looked in the mirror, watching himself lop off his beard, he was compelled to erase all remembrance of her, hoping it would take away the hurt he felt deep in the pit of his stomach.

When he'd cut as much as he could, he picked up his razor and shaved his chin thoughtfully, every stroke of the blade just as intentional as the one before it. He didn't stop until his chin was smooth.

He could be shunned for such an act of rebellion, but he didn't care. If it would keep him from having to attend Lydia's …

He closed his eyes against the thought of her funeral. He wasn't ready to say goodbye or let her go.

He dressed and shuffled his feet toward the door, wishing he didn't have to go through with this.

If he could bury his head in his pillow until the pain left him, he would. Sleep was the only way to keep his mind quiet of the thoughts that hurt so deeply.

Opening the door, he didn't expect Ellie to still be standing there waiting on him. She drew a hand to her mouth to stifle the gasp, but the look in her eyes spoke volumes of her shock at seeing his clean-shaven face.

"Not a word," he grumbled under his breath as he made his way to the waiting buggy.

His mother shared his sister's reaction, but she didn't say a word as he climbed in the open seat next to his brother-in-law. When they neared the graveyard, Eli choked up at seeing the entire community of buggies lined along the road. They had all gathered to pay their respects the same way they had when his father had passed on. His mother put a hand on his shoulder from behind him, but he was too inconsolable for it to comfort him.

Hannah felt awkward holding his child in his presence. He'd glanced at her briefly before climbing into the buggy, and she wondered if it was intentional. Had he wanted her to notice his clean-shaven face? She tried not to read too much into it, but had to wonder if he intended to follow through with the promise he'd made to Lydia. His mother had asked her to stay and care for the infant, and she'd agreed only for the child's sake. He was in no shape to take care of her, and from the way he reacted to her just now, it might be a permanent situation with her, and she would accept that.

In the two days that she'd cared for Mira, she admittedly had grown attached to her, despite every effort to guard her heart. She knew that if Eli didn't take over the care of his child soon, it would only be that much more difficult for her to separate herself from little Mira if he refused to honor his promise. Being the closest thing she'd likely ever get to having a *boppli* of her own, she considered offering to stay on as nanny to the child if that was all he would offer, and despite how tough it would be if she had to let go, she'd prayed for God's will.

Jonas parked the buggy, and hopped down to help the women out. Eli stared at the ground, allowing Ellie to take hold of Mira so Hannah could get out. She extended the child toward her brother, but he shook his head, his mouth forming a deep frown as he continued to keep his eyes cast down.

She sighed heavily, showing disapproval of her brother's reaction, but decided to let it go for now. Rather than say something she might regret, she prayed he'd bond with the child before she became too attached to Hannah, and she to the child.

She handed the baby back to Hannah, and urged her to walk beside her brother. It was proper for him to have his child at his side during the service, but she wasn't so sure about Hannah's presence—especially given her brother's clean-shaven face. She imagined the Bishop would take that as a sign he was willing to accept Hannah as a wife, and would likely expect him to marry her. Still, he should have waited to shave until a respectable amount of time had passed.

It was too late for all of that now.

Chapter 4

"I think you should marry Hannah the way you promised Lydia."

The Bishop's statement was more than mere suggestion, and Eli knew it.

The *only* reason he would even consider such a thing would be to make sure she continued to take care of the child. She would have to understand that he would never be a husband to her, but he doubted she would ever agree to it.

He would ask her just the same.

He knew the Bishop would not accept her continuing to live on his property without a marriage between them, even though he would stay in the *dawdi haus,* but he needed her to take care of the *boppli.* She would be nothing more to him than a nanny, and someone to cook for him and wash his clothes.

He put down the plate of food he had no intention of eating now. He couldn't believe he was even entertaining such thoughts when he'd just put his wife to rest less than an hour ago, but he had no other option if he wanted Hannah to stay on to take care of the child.

How could he honor such a promise when his heart would never be in it. He and Hannah had a history, and she'd want a regular marriage. As his friend, she deserved nothing less than that, but he wasn't the one to give her that.

The Bishop had strictly warned him they would have to be married immediately, or she would have to leave his home. Could he let her take the child—Lydia's child?

No; that was out of the question.

But so was a marriage for anything other than convenience. He would never betray Lydia's place in his heart by opening up to another woman in her stead, and he could never be anything more than friends with Hannah.

He glanced at her from the other side of the living-room of the Hochstetler's home where they'd gathered for the post-funeral meal. They weren't Lydia's family, but they were the closest thing she had to a real family; she'd come to stay with the older couple when she'd moved to the community. *Frau* Hochstetler had been friends with Lydia's *mamm,* and so when the woman passed away, she'd moved here with them. It had been Eli's luck, or so he thought.

Now, all he could think about was wishing he'd never met her so he wouldn't have to endure the pain of losing her. Was it right to wish for such a selfish thing? His jaw clenched as he looked away from the woman, who was not his wife, holding his child. He was supposed to share that child with the love of his life. Now all he felt was empty and broken. His faith was weak, and his heart ached with a deep sadness he hadn't even felt when his own father had passed away.

Though he knew he was obligated to marry Hannah, he felt nothing short of pure terror at the thought of it.

"I'll make all the arrangements," the Bishop was saying.

What? Had he missed an entire conversation just now?

He looked at Bishop Troyer blankly.

"I'm sure the Hochstetler's will be more than happy to accommodate the wedding. They cared for Lydia a great deal, and would want to make certain you and her *boppli* were well-cared for. Hannah will make an excellent *fraa.* In time, you'll heal, and be able to love her."

Eli put a hand to his mouth to cover the bile he thought was sure would escape him if he didn't stifle it.

Breathe, just breathe, he said to himself.

"My suggestion is that we *handle* it before the end of the week," he continued, despite Eli's apparent aversion to the subject. "Any longer than that and you'll have to either move from your farm, or move her off the property. It won't be considered proper after that, except that we know you're staying in the *dawdi haus."*

How? Did either Ellie or Hannah tell you my business?

Either way, he wasn't ready to think about getting married in front of the entire community. He'd just buried his wife, and already the Bishop was deciding and planning for his future wedding. He knew it was the way of the *Ordnung,* but that didn't mean he had to accept it, did it?

He supposed it did if he intended to remain in the community.

The real question weighing on his mind was; did he want to remain in the community?

He supposed he did if he wanted to have a mother for the child Lydia had left behind.

Chapter 5

Eli felt numb as he tried to react appropriately as the entire community either hugged him or shook his hand, offering condolences and raving about what a beautiful gift Lydia had left behind in Mira.

Guilt tugged at his heart every time a comment was made about the child. He hadn't set eyes on her since the moment she was born. He'd been too preoccupied with Lydia's passing to notice too much about the infant, but he had heard her all day at the funeral. She'd cried and cooed, and slept soundly, though he was very aware of her soft breathing even from across the room.

Was that his only connection to her? Lydia would likely have called it intuition, but to him, it only served as a grim reminder of his loss.

He knew what was expected of him, and he wasn't sure if he could go through with it.

When everyone had left, his *mamm* approached him and pulled him into an awkward hug. He feared really hugging her back because he knew it would cause him to breakdown, and he wasn't ready to face the emotions that had plagued him since his *fraa* had taken her last breath.

"I know this is a difficult time for you," she said quietly. "But you need to think of the *boppli* now. She's not Hannah's responsibility—unless you do what's right and marry her. I understand your reluctance to bond with Mira, because I imagine she reminds you too much of Lydia, but that's not fair to the wee one."

She knew him well; he couldn't deny that.

He wanted to collapse in her arms and cry like a child, but he clenched his jaw instead, stifling his emotions that begged to be let loose. It tortured him, despite his attempts to get past his obligations. He longed for the end of the day when he could collapse onto the bed in the *dawdi haus* when he could sleep away his grief.

"Do you want me to talk to her for you?" his *mamm* asked.

"I can't be a husband to her the way she deserves," he confessed, feeling a large weight lift from him.

"I know," she whispered. "You can't do it on your own, but *Gott* will help you."

"I *can't,"* he said weakly.

"Each day will get easier. You and I have something in common now, and I understand your heart is breaking. I had the luxury of being able to grieve, but you have to think of Lydia's *boppli: your boppli.* She loved that *boppli,* and that was her gift she left behind for you. When the breaking in your heart begins to lift, you'll be able to hold her and protect her the way your *fraa* made you promise. You *must* do this for her; it was her last wish for you and her *kinner."*

He understood what his *mamm* was trying to say; it made sense to him, but his heart would not cooperate. He could feel the emotion rising up in him, trying to escape. The tears filled his eyes and his throat constricted, his breath hitched and he clenched his jaw to stop it, but it was too late. Tears poured from his eyes despite every attempt to stifle them. He evened out his breathing trying his best to keep the others in the room from knowing what they could not see with his back turned to them. His mother had a way about her that continued to bring it out. She wept as she held him close, and he was comforted by her sobs that covered up his own sorrowful tears that continued to spill uncontrollably.

For some minutes, he wept alongside his mother, letting her embrace beget more tears from him than he ever thought he had in him. Before he could break free, Ellie had covered the two of them with her arms, and soon Jonas was among them, praying quietly. Bishop Troyer laid his hands on them and prayed, while he encouraged Hannah to join them, but she shook her head and cast her eyes to the ground.

She would wait for Eli to come to her on his own terms, whatever they may be. She would not take advantage of his grief. She'd made that mistake once and it had almost cost her the friends that now stood by Eli's side comforting him. She didn't belong there—not yet anyway. Her turn would come, but today was not that day. Eli needed time to recover his loss, and she would wait on him and the Lord to make her decision. If Mira was to be her child, she would wait on the Lord for a sure sign.

Though she felt a prompting from the Lord to be patient and wait on him, she was tempted to bolt from the house. Her nerves had been spent, and her heart was near-breaking. Her faith made her stay; she would stay until God told her to go, but she prayed faithfully that he would not make her. She loved Mira already, and she would love Eli if the Lord told her to do so, and she would marry him, even if it was only a marriage of convenience. She had been willing to marry Jonas for lesser reasons, but Eli and Mira were a whole different story. They needed her just as much as she needed them, and for that reason, she would wait. She would wait on God, and she would wait on Eli, no matter how long he asked her to.

Lord, speed his healing, and mend his heart. Give him a heart for his dochder, and for me, if it be your will. Bless me with the strength to wait until you give me your blessing, and the grace to accept if your answer is no.

Her prayer surprised her; she hadn't expected it, and when she opened her eyes, Eli was standing before her.

Had he heard her whisper of a prayer?

She waited for him to hold out his arms to his child, but he wouldn't even look at her tiny sleeping form resting her head on Hannah's shoulder.

"I'd like to talk to you in private," was all he said and then walked toward the front door.

Was she supposed to follow him?

Before she could make up her mind, Ellie was extending her arms to relieve her of the *boppli.* Her throat tightened and she kissed the top of her head, breathing her in as if it was the last time she might hold her.

With shaky hands she turned over the child to Ellie and reluctantly went to meet Eli to discover the fate of her future.

Chapter 6

Eli pulled in a deep breath, and paced the width of the driveway while he waited for Hannah to join him. He had no idea what he was going to say to her, or how he would go about convincing her that his plan was to her benefit. He'd seen in her eyes how attached she was to his daughter, and he prayed that would be enough to convince her to accept his proposal on his terms. He knew that it wasn't fair to ask such a thing, and that it could destroy their friendship, but his only concern at the moment was to provide for the child by giving her a mother. He was not prepared to take care of the child, and he had no idea if he would ever develop a fatherly instinct for her the way that Lydia had hoped.

Guilt tugged at his heart, as he realized he was letting Lydia down. She had wanted a real family for her child, and that was why she'd made him promise to marry Hannah in the first place. He swallowed hard as he realized she'd walked up behind him and was waiting for him to speak his peace.

Right away, he noticed that she'd left the child inside the house with his family. He was grateful for that, knowing it would be easier on him if he didn't have to see her. He already felt guilty enough for not being the father that his wife had wanted him to be.

He looked Hannah in the eye, pausing as he searched for the right words; even though he had no idea what he was going to say to her, but at least he was able to concentrate better without the distraction of the child.

He opened his mouth to speak, but the words would not come. He didn't want to marry Hannah for too many reasons; the biggest of these being that he'd just buried his wife. But the truth of the matter was, Mira needed a mother, and he knew he was not up to the task. Was it right to use his child as a lure for a marriage of convenience? He knew Hannah's desire to have a child of her own, and he felt he was taking advantage of her, but having a chance to be a mother was all he could offer her.

Hannah shifted from one foot to the other, wondering if she should just let Eli off the hook. “I’d like to offer my services as a nanny,” she began.

“Nee,” he interrupted her. “The Bishop will not allow you to remain on my property overnight to care for the *boppli* unless…”

He couldn’t finish the sentence.

“You don’t have to marry me, Eli,” she said gently. “I know this must be painful for you. I wish I could make this easy for you.”

He cleared his throat, hoping it would steady his voice, but his stomach clenched, resisting the words he had to get out before he lost his nerve.

“There is a way. You can accept a marriage of *convenience* with me in order to be the *boppli’s mamm.”*

“Jah,” she said softly. “I can do that.”

It wasn’t exactly what she wanted for her future, but she didn’t dare delay her answer for fear he would change his mind. If it meant she would be a *mamm,* she would be content with what she could get. Having a marriage of convenience and a *boppli* was better than being a childless spinster.

"I value your friendship, Hannah, and so did *Lydia,"* he said with a catch to his voice. "I know how difficult this is for you, but I need you to understand I won't be able to be a *husband* to you, and I won't be able to give you any *kinner* of your own."

His words were final. It was a reality she'd faced when she stepped aside for Ellie to marry Jonas, and now she was faced with it once again. But this time was different; this time, the offer came with a *boppli* but no real husband attached to it. Could she really accept such a thing and be happy? She thought of how empty her arms already felt without little Mira in them, and decided it would have to do.

"I understand," she said softly.

"I'll continue to live in the *dawdi haus,"* he said. "You can move your things into the main bedroom so you'll be across the hall from the *boppli."*

He was going to let her stay in his bedroom? What if he changed his mind later and wanted to move back in his house? She supposed she could move into one of the other rooms in the house, but she didn't understand why he didn't want her to stay where she was, except that it was now Mira's room. He'd moved the cradle into that room between the queen-size bed and the full-size crib, making the room even more crowded, but she supposed if he was moving her into the main bedroom—the room he'd shared with his wife, she would have plenty of room to put the cradle in there. Hannah didn't understand his reasoning for moving her, other than the fact he might not understand the immediate need to have the baby sleeping close in the cradle for the first couple of weeks. She wasn't about to argue with him or tell him how to handle his own home.

At this point, she felt blessed to have a home, a *boppli,* and a husband—even if in name only.

Chapter 7

Eli tried his best to be quiet as he packed up his bedroom to make it ready for Hannah. If it were up to him, he'd seal up the room and never deal with the memory of losing his wife here, but he knew that wasn't exactly being realistic. He didn't want to be in the room, and he didn't want to move Lydia's things, but they were of no use to her now, and seeing them would only be a reminder she was gone. He intended to pack them away quickly in the attic, and never see them again. He would be married in the morning to Hannah, and he would make her as comfortable as possible in his home. It was the least he could do for her, given the burden of a loveless marriage he had contracted with her.

She would never be his *bride,* only the caretaker for the child he could not be a father to.

He wasn't exactly sure what it was that made the situation so difficult, but he could only deal with one problem at a time, and that was to somehow get over his wife's death. Perhaps once his heart healed, there would be room for the child, but right now he didn't feel there was.

He'd prayed hard that first night; he'd prayed until he'd fallen asleep from sheer exhaustion, but he never felt the peace that he sought. Sadly, even now, he was not able to set his gaze upon the child, for fear he would break down. His heart ached, and his soul felt empty. He didn't think he would ever be the same again, and now he understood his own *mamm's* feelings of despair since his *daed's* death. She had tried to tell him that each day would get easier, and it wouldn't always be this way, but right at the moment he wasn't sure he believed that.

After haphazardly packing up everything he could get his hands on, and stuffing it into the cedar trunk he'd brought down from the attic, Eli thoughtfully lifted his wife's nightgown from the peg on the wall where she'd left it the night before she'd died. He drew it to his face, burying his nose in it, and breathing in her scent that still lingered on the garment. Perhaps this piece, he would set aside and keep with him for a time. He closed his eyes, trying to fool himself into believing she was still with him, but he just couldn't make it so. Emotion drew up in his throat, and before he realized, he was sobbing into her white linen nightgown. Uncontrollable sobs forced him to the floor, where he began to pray for deliverance of the pain and emptiness that now consumed him.

From across the hall, in Mira's room, Hannah could hear Eli sobbing, and wondered if he was trying to say goodbye to Lydia. She knew that letting go of his emotions would help him heal, but it brought tears to her eyes to listen to him. She felt bad, and wanted to go to him, but she didn't want to interfere or overwhelm him. She knew that marrying her was the last thing he wanted to do, but she respected him for honoring Lydia's dying wish for Mira.

Dropping to her knees beside the cradle, she placed a hand on the sleeping baby and began to pray.

Danki, dear Lord for finally blessing me with a boppli. Help me to be a good fraa to Eli, and give him the strength to overcome his loss. Bless him with a love for his boppli so she can grow up knowing her vadder. Give me the strength to be patient with him in this unsure time, and to step aside if need-be to allow him time with Mira.

Wiping fresh tears from her eyes, a deafening crash from the other room startled her from her prayer. The raucous continued, followed by low grumbling, but she couldn't quite make out his muffled words.

He was angry.

As a midwife, she was familiar with the stages of grief, and he was certainly exercising his discontent with his wife's death. Thankfully, Mira slept soundly, oblivious to the turmoil in her home.

Another crash rent the quiet night; she had her work cut out for her if he didn't clean up the messes he was now making. The noises moved to the hall, where it sounded as if he was dragging the furniture from the room. She didn't dare poke her head out into the hallway to see for herself, but she could only imagine that he was clearing the room of anything that would remotely remind him of his wife. When he'd offered the room to her, she wanted to tell him she was content to remain where she was, but she didn't want to start off her marriage by undermining whatever efforts he would make to accommodate her in his home.

More noise and another loud crash woke Mira. Hannah tried to pick her up before she let out a scream, but she wasn't successful. She rocked her and whispered to her it was alright, holding her close, hoping it would console her, but it would seem she was ready for another bottle. She would give anything if she didn't have to go out into the hall and face Eli in his state of grief, but it seemed inevitable.

Before she reached the door, he knocked lightly and let himself in. "I heard the crying," he began with downcast eyes. "I would like to move the furniture—perhaps while you feed her."

She didn't want to question him, so she simply nodded and walked past him to go down to the kitchen. She hadn't missed his puffy, red eyes that he'd tried to hide. Her heart ached for him, but she was powerless to help him. She would be supportive, but he would have to walk this journey alone for the most part. Though she wished she could relieve him from all of his hurt, he would have to feel it and work his way through it, while she supported him in the background—perhaps without his knowledge. She would never overstep her boundaries with him, but she would do everything she could to make his life easier.

As she reached the landing at the bottom of the stairs, she could hear him dragging what sounded like the bed from Mira's room across the hall to his bedroom. She felt funny taking the room from him, but she supposed he had no desire to sleep in there anymore. She only wished he wasn't determined to live in the *dawdi haus* even after their *wedding*.

She knew it wasn't a real marriage, or that he would want to share a room with her, but she would feel safer if he was in the main house. It had been too quiet the last few nights, except for the soft breaths from Mira in the cradle next to her. If not for that, she'd have been full of anxiety, she was certain. She wasn't used to being alone in a house, but she was prepared to get used to it. She wouldn't back out of the agreement now with Eli—not just because she didn't want to live alone. She'd chosen to be Mira's mother, and it was a sacrifice she would make for her.

Hannah hummed to Mira while she heated the goat's milk on the stove for her bottle. Upstairs, Eli continued to make noise, and she was determined not to go back up there until he came down. She felt terrible about what he was doing; she knew he was only trying to accommodate her, and it made her feel like she was putting him out. The last thing she wanted was for him to feel uncomfortable in his own home, but he'd made the decision to move into the *dawdi haus*. He'd also made the decision to marry her, and there would be no turning back now. The two of them would be the only ones who had to know it was a marriage of convenience only, and she would do her best not to let the situation be known to anyone else for fear it could compromise his standing in the community. She would honor him as if she was a real wife, even if it could never be.

Chapter 8

Eli wrung his hands as he cringed through the two-hour ceremony that now tied him to Hannah for the rest of his life. He thought about that for a moment, and wondered if he could endure being a widower again. He hadn't thought it would happen to him and Lydia, but here he was, marrying another woman just three days after her death. He regretted making the promise to her, wondering if he hadn't, if she would still be alive. Had she given up because she was content that he and the child would be taken care of in her absence? Had it been his promise that had caused her to let go of this life?

Hannah glanced over at Eli, ignoring the words being spoken by the Bishop, and wondering how other couples managed to stand through the lengthy ceremony. Were they all so in love that the time flew by? For her, it dragged on relentlessly as she worried with each sour expression from Eli that he was about to speak up and put an end to their wedding vows.

If he changed his mind before the Bishop finished, it would humiliate her beyond all reason, and she would lose her only chance at being a mother. She would never be able to live in the community and watch Mira grow up without being able to be her *mamm.*

She lifted her eyes and ran a prayer through her mind, continuing to drown out the Bishop's words that didn't really apply to her since she wasn't really going to be married after all was said and done—at least not in the biblical sense.

Danki Lydia for trusting me to be a mamm to your boppli, she prayed silently. *Please give your husband the strength to go through with this marriage to me. I'll do my best to take care of him and your wee one the same way you would, and I promise I'll make you proud...if you just keep me from being humiliated right now. Whisper in his ear that it's alright to marry me...whisper to him from Heaven...*

Her thoughts drifted back to the Bishop as he finished the ceremony, uniting the two of them until death parted them. She let out a sigh of relief that he was bound to her now, and that she would indeed be Mira's *mamm.* Tears welled up in her throat as the reality of it hit her.

She was a *mamm.*

Never mind that she was also a *fraa,* because she knew it could never be more than a marriage of necessity.

Eli excused himself immediately after the Bishop announced them, leaving Hannah to deal with the sympathetic stares that would surely be followed by a lot of gossip. She ignored the watchful eyes of the single women in the community, feeling awkward at best, but her main concern was Mira, who could be heard crying, and she thought for a moment Eli might go to her, but he walked past her and his family as he disappeared into the *dawdi haus.* He'd insisted that the wedding take place at his home, and now she understood why. She supposed he deserved his solace; after all, he'd had to force himself to marry her, and she knew that. It didn't make her feel any better about the situation, but surely the community had some understanding for him and his time of grief. She was simply going to be grateful he went through with the ceremony, and not worry about him. She would give him all the space he needed, and she would concentrate on taking care of Mira. After all, that's the only reason he married her.

Hannah went to the baby, and her new mother-in-law handed the baby over to her and kissed her on the cheek. "*Wilkum* to the *familye,*" she said to Hannah. "I know the circumstances aren't the best, but in time, Eli will open his heart to you."

She hadn't thought of that. Would he *eventually* expect her to be a proper wife in every way to him? She'd been willing to accept that when she planned to marry Jonas, but she'd had time to court him and was close enough friends with him to consider it. With Eli, they hadn't had many dates before Lydia came along and stole his affections away from her. The thought of it pricked her heart; had she loved him more than she'd allowed herself to admit?

Holding fast to Mira, she made her way into the kitchen to warm up some milk for a bottle, her mother-in-law on her heels. Thinking back on the times she'd spent with the woman after Ellie had left for her *rumspringa*, was it possible she'd felt cheated that Eli had recently married Lydia? A strange feeling welled up in her, and she pushed it down.

Frau Yoder put a hand on Hannah's shoulder, startling her from her reverie. "You seem suddenly troubled. Did I say the wrong thing out there in the yard?"

Hannah waited for some of the ladies to gather their dishes of food from the oven and go outside to the tables that were set up for the wedding meal.

"*Nee,*" she said quietly. "I believe I was just thinking about everything and I got a little overwhelmed."

She could not confide in Eli's mother that she'd just realized she loved him, and had been suppressing it for almost two years. Or perhaps she'd felt the rush of love when he'd whooshed by her after their vows had been spoken? Whichever it was, it didn't matter. She loved Eli—her new husband, and she would wait patiently for him to return that love.

Chapter 9

Eli walked into the kitchen in the midst of all the women guests for the wedding dinner feeling as awkward as he could be. He heard whispers, but ignored them despite the strong urge to make them leave his home. The last thing he wanted was to be the subject of gossip among the women in the community. He knew they expected him to stay close to Hannah's side, but he wanted to go back to the *dawdi haus* and hide until the day was over and everyone went home. But that was not what was expected of him, and he knew he had to at least go through the motions. Surely he could get through one day. After that, he could go back to the solitude of the *dawdi haus* where his heart was safe from breaking. He glanced at Hannah, who managed a weak smile, but he couldn't return it.

His *mamm* pulled him into a hug and drew him into the other room, while Hannah stayed behind, trying desperately not to cry in front of her guests. Thankfully, her younger sister, Rachel, stayed close to her the entire day—mostly because she was so enamored with Mira.

"Now that you're a *mamm,* are you going to let me come over and help you with the *boppli?"*

"Jah," Hannah replied. "You know you're always *wilkum* here."

She handed the sleeping baby over to her sister so she could remove the rolls from the oven. She felt awkward, even though this was her house and her kitchen now, but she could feel the eyes on her backside of women she used to count as friends. Some of them were jealous because Eli had been for two days the most eligible catch in the community in a while. Some were simply nosy, busy-bodies who loved nothing more than to have something to talk about to spice up their own dull lives.

"Can you please excuse me?" Rachel said to them. "I need a private moment with *mei schweschder."*

Hannah felt a spark of relief as she kept her back to the women while they filed out through the kitchen door and out into the yard. She watched them from the kitchen window, their expressions unhappy, as they seemed to be voicing their dislike for being ushered out of the house by a teen.

She turned around and suppressed a giggle.

"*Danki* for rescuing me from that awkwardness," she whispered to Rachel. "I couldn't take their stares or their whispering for another minute!"

"Your marriage is none of their business. It's between you and Eli. I heard some of the stuff they were saying. Is it true you're only married to him to take care of the *boppli?"*

Hannah searched for the best words to explain to her little sister. "For now," she said. "Until his heart heals."

"I heard them saying he won't go anywhere near his own *boppli."*

"He's grieving right now, Rachel. Sometimes, when adults are grieving, they need time to get over that hurt before they can spend too much time with others. He loves Mira, or he wouldn't have married me so she could have a *mamm.* It was a great sacrifice for him to marry me when he's still grieving the way he is, but he did what was best for her."

"So you're not really his *fraa?"*

"Nee," Hannah said sadly. "At least not the way I would be if he was in love with me."

"But you love him, don't you?" she asked.

She cast her eyes down, hiding the blush at her naïve sister's comment.

"Does he know that you love him?"

"*Nee*," Hannah said quietly. "He isn't ready to know that yet."

Ellie walked into the kitchen just then with little Katie who was fussing. "I hope I'm not banned from the house like Naomi and her friends," she said with a chuckle.

"Is that what they said?" Rachel asked. "*Busy-bodies*!"

"Rachel would you mind taking Katie up to Mira's room with you and putting her down for a nap?"

She rolled her eyes. "I can take a hint."

"*Danki*," Hannah called after her as she left the room.

Ellie pulled Hannah into a hug. "We are sisters now."

Hannah began to weep quietly onto her friend's shoulder. "*Ach,* it wasn't supposed to happen this way."

"I know, and I'm sorry, but I know how much you love my brother. I never really got to know Lydia since I was gone right after their wedding, but you, I do know, and I know what a big heart you have. If anyone can help Eli get his heart back and be a father to Mira, I know you can."

"*Danki,* that means a lot to me."

Ellie pulled away and smiled. "Don't cry anymore; it's your wedding day."

She sniffled. "It wasn't a *real* wedding."

Ellie scrunched her brow. "Of course it was. You'll see, my brother will come to love you just as soon as he's had time to process everything. He'll appreciate you being here for him and for his *dochder*—for your *dochder* now. You and I are sisters now and we are both *mamms,* and Katie has a new cousin. Be happy. It will all work out; God has a plan for you and your new family."

Hannah wiped her tears and forced a smile, just as Eli and his *mamm* entered the room.

He held a shaky hand out to her. "Let's go out and eat with our guests."

Hannah placed her hand in his, the warmth of his skin making her flesh tingle well past her elbow. She followed him out into the yard, where it was evident by their expressions that she was the envy of all the single women in the community.

Chapter 10

Eli stepped into the kitchen with a fresh pail of goat's milk for the *boppli.* He intended to milk the goat for Hannah to keep her out of the barn as much as possible, in order to avoid having to make small talk with her that felt forced and uncomfortable. She stood at the stove dishing up scrambled eggs and bacon onto a plate, and turned when he entered the room.

He paused, feeling awkward when she handed him the food.

She was being kind to him—being a wife—and he didn't like it. It only made him feel even more guilty that he could not be a husband to her the way she deserved. He cared for her, but he would not allow himself to love her, for fear it would betray his wife's memory.

It was only a meal, and she'd made it for him willingly. He owed her nothing for it. After all, he was providing her with a home, and had basically given his child to her. He grumbled a *Danki* under his breath, and took the plate of food out to the *dawdi haus* to eat it. He hated seeming rude and ungrateful, but he was not up for socializing with her.

She'd not said a word to stop him from leaving the house, and he preferred it that way. Having to keep up appearances yesterday at the wedding meal had exhausted him to the point he almost couldn't get out of bed this morning, but he knew that keeping himself busy on his farm would also keep his mind too busy to dwell on his grief.

With Eli out of the house, Hannah sat at the kitchen table alone and choked down the meal around the lump in her throat. She knew he hadn't meant to hurt her feelings, and so she forgave him, but that didn't mean it didn't hurt anyway. If it was possible, she almost felt more lonely married than she had when she was single.

She rose from the table and went to the sink with her dishes. Looking out at the *dawdi haus,* she knew she'd have to go in there after he returned to the barn to resume his chores to get his dirty dishes and clothes. She would continue to cook and clean for him, and take care of his child, hoping that someday he would return her love. If he didn't, she prayed God would remove the love in her heart for him to keep her heart from breaking. She feared her love would continue to grow for him and he would never let himself love her back.

After running water in the sink, she heard Mira crying in her cradle in the other room. Hannah had brought it downstairs so she could cook, not wanting to be out of earshot of the infant. She wondered how new mothers managed to get anything done; so far, she had a lot of things started, but nothing finished—unless she counted the morning meal, but that was nothing short of a disaster.

She went to her child and changed her diaper, then held her close and kissed her, feeling ashamed for complaining the least little bit about her husband. Though he might not ever be ready to be a husband in the traditional sense, he'd given her the best gift a man could give a woman; he'd given her a child to care for and love, and that was a far better life than she would have had if Eli hadn't rescued her from becoming a spinster.

As she prepared Mira's bottle, she reflected on a prayer she'd prayed not too long ago asking God to bless her with a husband. He'd not only blessed her with a husband, but a child too. But was it all part of God's plan for Lydia to have to pass away in order for her to get what she wanted in life? Tears welled up in her eyes as she thought about it.

Dear Lord, did my prayers bring Lydia's death? Forgive me if my prayers were selfish.

Deep down, she knew better, and she was determined she wouldn't waste even a day of the blessing God bestowed on her by dwelling on how it was He blessed her.

She feared if she gave in to such foolish notions it would increase the guilt that already weighed her down.

Chapter 11

Hannah fashioned a sling from a bed-sheet, wrapping Mira in it, and tying it close to her so she wouldn't have to lug around the laundry basket while trying to balance the *boppli* in her arms. With the wee one tucked against her heart, she pulled the ends of the sheet over both arms and crossed it over her shoulders, tying it at her waist. She prayed that hearing her heart, Mira would be soothed by it and get used to hearing it. It was a mother's heartbeat that soothed a fussy infant, and she hoped Mira would be comforted by it, and come to know it as her own *mamm*.

Though it was Saturday, Hannah was determined to get ahead of the laundry that had piled up for the past week, hoping to be finished by the end of the day on Monday. It was beginning to get a little chilly, being the second week of November, and so she placed a bonnet on Mira's head, assuming Lydia had crocheted it.

Heading out to the *dawdi haus,* her first stop would be to gather Eli's things. She worried he would think she was overstepping her boundaries, and so she prayed he wouldn't cross her path while she was in there.

He'd spent most of the day tinkering with something. All she knew was the constant sound of a hammer, and wondered what he could be building. Perhaps it was a new stall for the horse that was about to foal. With winter coming, it would need space inside the barn.

She had noticed that Lydia had not finished canning all of her vegetables, and she hoped Eli would not be upset if she finished the chore. She'd come across the unfinished task in the root cellar when she was searching for staples to prepare for the week's meals. She thought perhaps he wouldn't even notice, since he'd been avoiding her as much as possible.

With him spending so much time in the barn and living in the *dawdi haus*, it almost seemed comical to her that she felt more like a single mom than a married woman. She hoped that time would heal his wounds, and that he would begin to spend time with his daughter.

Even if he didn't want to see her or be a husband to her in any way, she prayed that he would begin to be a father to Mira.

Setting down the basket on the floor of the bedroom in the *dawdi haus*, Hannah began to strip the bed so she could change the linens. She almost missed the nightgown that was tucked under his pillow, and realized it belonged to Lydia. Her heart ached at the thought of him pining over a dead woman, but she supposed it would take some time for him to recover from his loss. She couldn't imagine the sort of hurt he was feeling from losing someone so dear to him, but it wasn't because she hadn't experienced loss in her own life. Still, losing a spouse had to be much different than the loss of a parent or extended family such as a cousin.

She retrieved the nightgown from the laundry basket, and folded it neatly, placing it back under the pillow. Then, she proceeded to pick up his laundry from the hamper in the bathroom. Once she gathered all his things, she retrieved his dirty dishes from the sink in the kitchen and place them on top of the laundry in the basket. She hoisted the basket up onto her hip, and the dishes clanked, startling Mira, but she quickly relaxed again and didn't wake Fully.

Relieved, Hannah was careful to be quieter as she exited the *dawdi haus* out into the cold November air. She tucked the small knitted blanket over the baby's head and hands that stuck outside the sling to keep the cool air from giving her a chill. Hannah knew it wasn't too chilly for her, but babies were much more sensitive to the cold than adults were, and she aimed to guard her from the gusts of wind that threatened to bring snow from the Northern sky.

Once inside the main house, she went to the modern laundry room where she'd washed her clothes for the past couple of weeks that she'd stayed as a guest. Eli had done well for himself by installing a windmill and solar panels on the roof of the main house, the *dawdi haus*, and the barn. Those things provided enough electricity to run the home efficiently. And though she had a modern gas-powered dryer, she preferred to hang the wash outside, even in the cold crisp air of late autumn. She'd used the clothesline several times already, and had familiarized herself enough with where everything was in the home. Since she'd taken care of Lydia in her last days of her pregnancy, she was grateful she'd had that time to acclimate herself with the home. It made the transition easier now that she was the woman of the house.

Stopping in the kitchen to drop off the dishes in the sink, she took the time to run some hot water so they could soak. Eli had left them there since the previous morning, and he had not returned for another meal that day. After missing the noon meal, however, Hannah had slipped into the *dawdi haus* and put a plate of food in the refrigerator for him to have for dinner. She was happy to see that he'd used the dishes and he'd eaten the meal that she'd left for him. She knew that keeping up his strength was important right now. If she could help it, she would not allow him to become run-down. She would feed him well and continue to pray for him that strength and peace would get him through this tough time. She didn't enjoy invading his privacy, but it was necessary in order to keep him from wasting away and wallowing in his grief.

Eli took a break from building the stall in the barn, and decided to get himself a drink of water, and he needed to use the bathroom. As he entered the *dawdi haus*, he noticed that things had been moved. Hannah had been in here again, and left him feeling a bit invaded. When he walked into the bedroom, panic filled him when he saw the bare mattress. He rushed to the bed and dropped to his knees grabbing his pillow and pulling it to him. Then he noticed that Lydia's nightgown was still there. It was folded neatly, and had been replaced back under the pillow. Hannah had respected him enough to put it back where she'd found it, and that meant everything to him right now.

He breathed a sigh of relief as he pulled the garment toward him and buried his face in it, breathing a prayer that God would relieve him from his grief and to make him the sort of man Hannah could be proud to call a husband, and Mira could be proud to call him *vadder*.

Chapter 12

Hannah hadn't expected to run into Eli when she returned to the *dawdi haus* to change the bedding. With Mira still strapped to the front of her, and fresh linens in both arms, she hadn't thought about the need to knock on the door.

Taking him by surprise, Eli scrambled to his feet, trying to hide his embarrassment by wadding up the nightgown and stuffing it into the dresser drawer. He'd been so engrossed in prayer that he hadn't heard her approach. He didn't quite know why it mattered that she knew he had ahold of the garment, especially since she already knew it was there.

She immediately tried to excuse herself and back out of the room, but he was already awkwardly moving past her to get out of the house. As he brushed by her, he glanced down at the *boppli* laying against her, his expression quickly fell, his eyes cast down toward the floor.

Her arm tingled from the warmth of his bare forearm brushing against hers, and she was glad he'd left the room so he couldn't see her blushing now. She prayed he wasn't angry with her for barging in on him. she'd tried to apologize, but he didn't seem interested in hearing it; he seemed to preoccupied with getting away from her and Mira.

She swallowed the lump in her throat and asked God to keep her from taking it personally. She was certain the tufts of blond curls on Mira's head painfully reminded him of Lydia. She could see the pain in his eyes when he looked at the child.

Hannah set to work quickly to make the bed so she didn't have to invade his space any more than she had to. As for the nightgown; she would leave it in the drawer where he left it.

When she finished, Mira began to wake up, and she went back to the main house to get a bottle ready. Again, she ran into Eli, who had brought in a fresh pail of goat's milk for Mira.

"*Danki,*" she said softly.

He nodded, taking a long look at the infant before exiting the house.

At least he was able to really look at her this time, Hannah thought happily. *Danki, Lord, for small miracles.*

A knock at the door made her wonder if he'd forgotten something, but she didn't think he would knock on his own door, would he?

She hollered "*Kume,*" while she poured the milk into Mira's bottle.

The door opened behind her, and she turned to see who it was. Hannah fell back against the counter, dropping the bottle of milk when she caught herself from falling to the floor. Her heart sank as she gazed upon the *Englisch* woman.

"You must be Hannah," she said.

Lydia!

Hannah couldn't find her voice.

"I'm here for my sister's baby," she said, looking at Mira. "This must be her."

"*What?*" Hannah said.

Did she just say she was here for the boppli—as in to take her away? Did she say she was Lydia's schweschder?

Hannah was having a hard time looking past the identical resemblance to Lydia.

"My Mennonite cousins called me only yesterday, or I'd have been here sooner," she said, reaching for Mira.

Before she realized, the woman had managed to lift Mira from the bunting she'd had tied to her.

Hannah looked at her and quickly surveyed the door, wondering if the woman intended to really *take* Mira. Surely Eli would stop her, wouldn't he?

The woman looked at her and frowned. "I'm guessing you didn't know Lydia had a twin? I'm Alana. I've been shunned because I left after taking the baptism. The community wouldn't even let me attend my parent's funerals with the rest of the family. I wasn't allowed to attend my own sister's wedding, and now I've missed *her* funeral too, but they won't keep me from her baby!"

"I can't speak for *mei mann,* Eli," Hannah said, feeling suddenly vulnerable and threatened.

"Yes, I was told my sister's husband remarried two days ago!" she said, her lip curling up at the sight of Hannah. "What kind of man remarries so soon after his wife dies?"

"Your *schweschder* made him promise to marry me shortly after giving birth…so that Mira would have a *mamm,*" Hannah said defensively.

"*Mira?*" Alana asked. "Whose decision was it to name that child after my mother?"

"Lydia named the child. I was the midwife in attendance."

"So it's *your* fault my sister is dead!"

Tears welled up in Hannah's eyes. "*Nee,* Mira was breech, and Lydia was bleeding too much. By the time the ambulance arrived, she was already gone."

"Who called for the ambulance?" Alana asked.

"Eli and I *both* insisted, even though Lydia was against it."

"I was also told that Eli won't even have anything to do with my sister's baby," Alana continued.

Was she *looking* to find fault in order to give her a reason to take the child away?

"He's grieving," Hannah said, defending him.

"The child clearly needs a mother!"

Hannah pulled the fresh bottle of milk from the pan of hot water on the stove and tested the warmth against her wrist. Mira had begun to cry, and she held her arms out to take the child.

Alana snatched the bottle from her. "I'm perfectly capable of feeding my sister's baby!"

Hannah didn't say a word, but stayed close in case she didn't calm down in the stranger's arms.

She sat in a chair at the kitchen table and placed the bottle in Mira's mouth. She began to gulp it down.

"When's the last time you fed her?" Alana asked. "She's acting like she's starving!"

"She had a bottle a little over two hours ago," Hannah answered calmly.

Alana leaned down and kissed Mira's head, closing her eyes and smelling her head. "I should be the logical one to raise my sister's child—not a *stranger.*"

Mira looked content in Alana's arms, and it brought tears to Hannah's eyes. Was she going to attempt to take her away?

"I'm guessing since my sister's husband is living in the *dawdi haus,* the two of you haven't *consummated* your marriage."

Hannah hung her head out of embarrassment at the woman's forward statement.

"I didn't think so," Alana said. "In that case, I can go to the Bishop and have your marriage annulled."

Panic rose up in Hannah. Could she do that?

"I'll marry Eli and raise my sister's baby. After a lengthy confession, I'll be welcomed back into the community, and when I marry him, I won't be shunned anymore."

Just then, Eli walked into the door. He'd not wanted to enter the house and run into Hannah again, but he needed to find out who owned the car that was blocking him from leaving his driveway to go into town.

There in front of him was his child in the arms of…

His heart drummed against his ribs, and his breath caught in his throat. His legs felt suddenly wobbly as he stumbled forward, knocking over the chair in his path.

Lydia?

Chapter 13

Alana looked at the man in front of her, wondering about his clean-shaven face. Was this her sister's husband? If so, why had he dishonored his wife by shaving his beard? Was it because Hannah hadn't become his wife in the biblical sense?

Eli looked to Hannah, who looked just as befuddled as he was by the mysterious woman's presence. It was obvious to him that she was the twin sister his wife had mentioned a time or two during their short-lived courtship and marriage.

"Are you Alana?" he asked.

"Yes I am," she answered. "I'm guessing by your reaction to me that you must be Eli."

"Jah," he replied.

"We have a lot to talk about," she said. "Will you take me out to visit my sister's grave?"

He looked to Hannah. "Can you be ready to go so I can take her to the graveside?"

"I'd like to go with just you," Alana said.

"It wouldn't be proper to go without an escort," Eli said.

"Then we'll take Mira with us."

Hannah's heart sank. Was this woman about to take her whole world away from her?

"Nee," he replied. "She's *mei fraa."*

"That's exactly what I want to talk to you about," she said as she set Mira's bottle down and lifted her onto her shoulder to burp her.

Again, Eli looked to Hannah. "Are you ready to go?"

She would not argue with the man, but it was obvious Alana didn't want her to go. She nodded to him, deciding to obey her husband.

Grabbing Mira's knitted bonnet and sweater, she tried to coax the infant out from Alana's arms, but she merely held her hand out to take the knitted things. Hannah picked up the thick quilt and handed it to the woman while she put on her black cloak and bonnet.

"Maybe I should warm an extra bottle," she said, hoping to stall a little for time.

She didn't know why, but perhaps she hoped Eli would make her go alone once she left the room to make the bottle. Alana followed her, so that plan backfired on her.

"You'll need to move your car," he said to Alana.

"Why don't we just take my car?"

Hannah looked to Eli to give a quick excuse, and he didn't disappoint her.

"We don't have a car-seat for the *boppli,*" he said calmly.

She smiled. "I've got one! It'll be much faster if we take my car."

Hannah nodded slightly to him. She was all for getting this trip over with quickly and getting rid of Alana so she could be rid of her.

"I'll get my things out of the car while you put the horse and buggy away."

"Your *things?*" Hannah asked.

Alana looked around her. "Surely this house has an extra room that I could stay in."

Hannah kept quiet hoping Eli would tell her to leave, but this time he disappointed her.

"You're more than *wilkum* to stay here during your visit."

Then he disappeared to put away his horse.

She knew it was their way not to turn a relative away, but she was a shunned woman. Surely he wasn't going to let her stay on for an extended period of time—except that he wasn't there during that part of the conversation and didn't know what she'd said to her.

Surely he *had* to know, didn't he?

She would not be able to say anything now, and so she kept her mouth shut and went along with Alana pushing her around. It made her angry, but she would let it go until Eli fixed it.

With Eli and Alana both outside, she prayed that the woman would not come between her and her husband and child.

But then she had a thought.

Was it selfish of her to keep Mira away from her blood relative? Was it really better for Lydia's sister to raise her? Surely Lydia would have mentioned her with her dying breath and make Eli promise to marry Alana instead of her if she trusted her, wouldn't she? Perhaps she didn't trust her estranged sister, and for that reason, Hannah would keep a close eye on her.

Let your will be done, Lord, she prayed.

Chapter 14

Alana brought her suitcases into the house and dropped them on the floor beside the kitchen door. Then, she extended her arms out to Mira. "I'll put her in the car-seat."

Hannah let her take the baby from her. She reasoned that she was, after all, Mira's *aenti*. So she let it go—for now. Since Alana seemed a bit bossy, she had to wonder why it was that Lydia had not warned Eli about her. Had she forgotten about her when she was taking her last breath, or had she not thought her own sister would pose a threat to her daughter's future? Either way, Hannah had made a promise to Lydia that she would be a *mamm* to her *boppli,* and she was determined to protect her at all cost—even from her own *aenti.*

Eli took his time putting *Moose* in the barn, hoping by stalling, he could come up with a way to get Alana out of his mind. When he'd set his eyes on her, she'd taken his breath away. She looked so much like Lydia, it was tough for him to suppress the urge to pull her into his arms and make himself forget his wife was gone. But could he really fool himself like that for more than a few minutes?

Realizing what he was thinking, he dropped to his knees beside a large bale of hay. *Lord, forgive me for thinking about holding Alana when I'm married to Hannah. Help me to pull myself together and face Lydia's death before I destroy my future and the future of Hannah and Mira. Help me to figure a way out of the mess I'm in, and show me your plan for my life. Let your will be done, Lord.*

Once Mira was all strapped in, Eli came out of the barn, his expression heavy. Hannah climbed in next to the baby in the back seat, and Eli surprised her by getting in beside her.

"Wouldn't you feel more comfortable up front with me, Eli?" Alana asked. "It would give us a chance to talk."

"Nee," he said politely. "I can hear you just fine from back here, and I prefer to sit with *mei familye."*

He felt Hannah relax beside him, and her closeness sent a strange shiver through him. the warmth of her thigh that touched his made it tough for him to concentrate on anything else.

What was happening to him?

His emotions were all over the place.

He reasoned that it was because they were about to go to the graveside of his beloved Lydia, and he was simply still in shock from her death.

But it was more than that, and he knew it.

He was certain Hannah could sense it too.

Resting his elbow against the window, he leaned his chin on his palm and stared out the window as they passed farm after farm.

His neighbors.

The trees were nearly bare, and the miles of farmland was littered with colorful leaves. Winter would be upon them within days, and the snow would close them in for the season. Would he be able to bear the cold of the *dawdi haus?* It wasn't that the house lacked a fireplace, because it had a nice stone hearth. It was the lack of love and family that the place represented. He didn't like being all alone out there, and it would get even lonelier with a long winter separating him from his only child.

He let his gaze wander to Mira. She was truly a beautiful baby. Her curly blond hair reminded him of Lydia, and her blue eyes mirrored his own. He reached across Hannah and touched Mira's small hand. Her milky skin was warm enough to melt his heart.

He removed his hand, glancing at Hannah. Tears filled her eyes, and she smiled warmly at him. He forced a smile, but it wasn't as tough as he thought it was going to be.

Alana pulled into the cemetery with a loud sigh. "Which way?"

Eli pointed and told her the section marking to look for. She pulled into the lot beside the row of graves where Lydia was laid to rest. Turning around in her seat, she asked Eli to take her to the grave.

He placed a hand on Hannah's arm.

There was that strange shiver again.

"*Kume,*" he said to his wife.

She unbuckled Mira and lifted her into her arms, and slid across the seat to exit the car. She walked beside her husband as they made their way to the gravesite. It was an emotional setting that made Hannah feel uncomfortable.

Alana fell to the ground and began to weep, repeatedly apologizing to Lydia for not being there for her, while Eli worked his jaw to keep it clenched against the tears that would surely fall if he didn't keep his emotions in check.

Strong frigid winds brought dark clouds swiftly overhead, and Hannah worried icy rain would soon be upon them.

"Perhaps I should take the *boppli* back to the car out of the wind," Hannah said, interrupting Alana's confession to her sister.

Alana jumped up from the grave and wiped her eyes and looked at Eli. "I should go with her to help protect my sister's baby. I'll give you some time here, Eli."

He nodded and the two women headed toward the car. When they were nearly there, Alana stopped and handed Hannah the keys.

"You know, I forgot to leave a memento at my sister's grave. You get the baby in the car, and I'll be right back."

Hannah accepted the keys, though she was certain it was an excuse for Alana to converse with her husband about going to the Bishop regarding their marriage. After strapping Mira in the car-seat, she turned around and watched as the woman seemed to be deep in the middle of a long lecture with Eli.

After a few minutes, however, Eli nodded to her and began to walk away, and it appeared to anger Alana, who followed closely on his heels, apparently chattering about her plans to get her way.

Hannah felt a sharp pain at her ribcage, heartburn souring her stomach over the woman's actions. It seemed she was determined to have her cause heard, and she didn't seem like the type to back down. Worry turned to fear in Hannah's stomach, but Eli's expression remained calm as he slid into the back seat of Alana's car next to her. She looked to her husband for comfort, and he gave it to her with a simple gesture.

He placed his hand on top of hers, tapping lightly only twice before removing it, but it was enough to let her know he was not going to stand for Lydia's sister getting in the way of her last wishes for her family.

Chapter 15

They rode back to the house in silence, and Hannah's heart beat faster the closer they came to the farm she wasn't sure she'd be calling *home* very much longer if Alana had any say in it.

Eli unexpectedly took Mira from Hannah and walked into the house with the two of them, and then handed her back once they got inside the kitchen. Reaching down, he picked up Alana's bags and began to walk outside with them.

"Where are you taking my things?" she asked impatiently. "I plan on staying here."

He turned and looked her in the eye. "You can stay in the *dawdi haus.*"

She twisted up her face and planted her hands on her hips in a huff. "I'm not living out there with you. We aren't married yet!"

"We aren't going to be married because I'm already married—to Hannah. And I won't be living out there either; I'm moving *mei* things back in the main *haus* with *mei familye.*"

Hannah's heart thumped harder at the thought of Eli being in the house with her. Surely he intended to sleep in one of the four bedrooms upstairs—unless he decided he wanted to move her out of his own room so he could return to it. Either way, she would accommodate him; after all, it was *his* house.

"That isn't going to stop me from going to see the Bishop in the morning!" she called after him.

Eli kept walking with her bags, set them inside the door and haphazardly tossed his few things on top of the bed, wrapped it up in his quilt, and grabbed his pillow with his other hand.

"I'll send Hannah out with some clean linens and towels for you," he said as he took his things from the bathroom. Luckily, he hadn't moved his things fully into the small cottage, or it would have been much too time-consuming to gather his things, and he intended not to make another trip out to the *dawdi haus*. He wouldn't step foot back in the place until Alana was long-gone, and he hoped that would be soon.

It wasn't that he intended to keep her from seeing her niece, but if she meant trouble for his wife or child, he would have no other choice but to make her leave. A sudden rush of responsibility washed over him, leaving him feeling strange about his change of heart where Hannah and Mira were concerned. He knew deep down it was his duty to protect them. He felt compelled to in such a strong way—a way that almost made him think he loved them both.

He entered the main house, his arms full. Walking past Hannah, he went up the stairs and hesitated before going into the room he shared with Lydia. It seemed like an entire lifetime ago that he was in that room with her holding her hand as she slipped away from him, but now, as he entered the room; he didn't recognize any of it.

Everything was different.

In the corner, Mira's cradle rested on a braided rug he didn't recognize. Doilies and late-blooming wild flowers propped in Mason jars rested on both lamp tables, fancy oil lamps in place of the copper ones that were there before. In general, the room looked *feminine,* but he set his things on top of the yellow and white wedding-ring quilt he figured Hannah must have sewn for her dowry. All in all, the room was fresh and sunny in appearance, the yellows adding a cheerfulness to the room. It looked so different; he thought he might just be able to be comfortable in the room again.

Hannah entered the room just then with Mira asleep on her shoulder.

He looked at her holding his child and suddenly remembered what made him begin courting her at a time that seemed like a whole other lifetime ago. It was her big heart that appealed to him.

She set the baby in the cradle without a word to him, and then eyed his things on the bed. Immediately, she went to the dresser and began to remove her things from the drawer. "I'll have *mei* things packed quickly, but I'll need to have you move the cradle across the hall for me."

He walked over to her and placed a hand on hers, stopping her from packing. "I want you to stay."

Her breath hitched, and she bit her bottom lip. Surely he didn't mean what he said.

Chapter 16

Hannah wrung her hands nervously when Eli asked her to sit beside him on the bed. She knew he was her husband, and she didn't fear him, but she'd not been in this situation, and he'd been married before already.

"I know I said I would not be a husband to you in any way, but it seems Alana is challenging that. I hate to even ask to place such a burden on you, but I'm afraid until she leaves, we are going to have to make it *appear* that we are married in every sense of the way—if you understand my meaning."

He was being kind and she understood, but it made her nervous to put on pretenses. She nodded nonetheless.

"I'll need to stay in the room with you and Mira at night—but I'll sleep on the floor."

"That won't be necessary," she said. "I trust you."

He cleared his throat nervously. It was evident he wasn't through talking about the problem.

"She didn't just threaten to go to the Bishop; she mentioned talking to a lawyer. If you and I are not married in the traditional sense, she could pursue action to annul our marriage. At least that's what she claims. I don't think we need to consult a lawyer because she can't force me to marry her if I don't want to. I want you to know I'm dedicated to this marriage—even though it's only for convenience. I've watched you with Mira, and I believe Lydia made a wise choice when she asked you to be her *mamm.*"

His voice broke a little, and she knew it wasn't easy for him to talk about any of this.

"Danki," Hannah said softly.

"I need to know if it's alright with you if I act *affectionately* toward you around Alana so she gets the idea we are a *real couple.*"

"Jah, but do you really think that'll be necessary?"

He stood up and began to put his things away in the empty dresser that he was used to using before.

"I'm afraid Alana has become even more *Englisch* than Lydia described to me, and she isn't going to take our word for it. She's going to want to see for herself that she can't break up our *familye.*"

"Ach, I have a tough time understanding how she thinks she can come here and take over."

"Lydia was the last of her *familye,* and they were very close when they were *kinner* in the same *haus,* but Alana wanted to separate herself from her twin and be her own person. Lydia told me she always felt like she was her shadow, and she wanted the world to see *her* and not the two of them as one. It's not easy for me to understand either because Ellie and I are not identical twins. The only thing I do understand is the bond between twins, and I imagine it must be greater if the person is a clone of you. She believes because she is an identical replica of Lydia that she's the logical *replacement* for her, and that Mira will automatically bond with her because of it. I don't agree with that because they don't share the same heart."

He hung his head.

Hannah knew this was all too much too soon for him; it was for her too. Still, she would trust that he knew what was best—especially if it helped her to remain Mira's *mamm.*

Chapter 17

Hannah was happy to see Rachel when she showed up to help with the evening meal. Having finished her chores at home, she'd taken the extra time to lend a hand where it was greatly needed. Not to mention the fact she knew she would feel less intimidated by Alana with her sister around. Rachel was, after all, far more outgoing than Hannah was herself, and if Alana spoke out of turn, Rachel would be the one to put her in her place. She'd always been a little mouthy that way, but she supposed it was more because of the cousins she was always hanging around. That, and her young age.

Lately, she and her cousins had talked non-stop about taking their *rumspringa*, and Hannah dreaded the thought of it for her younger sister, whom she worried would not return if she got a taste of *Englisch* freedom, as she referred to her upcoming right-of-passage. With her birthday just around the corner, Hannah hoped that spending extra time with her and Mira would make her crave a future as an Amish wife rather than the wild and rule-free life of the *Englisch.*

"Whose car is that outside?" she asked as she bound in the door and went straight to the infant seat to pick up the baby.

"It belongs to Alana—Lydia's twin sister. She's here to cause trouble for me, so I'm glad you're here. I don't trust her."

Hannah handed her sister the baby's bottle so she could feed Mira while she finished putting her pie in the oven.

"What sort of trouble?" Rachel asked.

She wiped her hands on her apron and sat across from Rachel at the kitchen table.

"She caused Eli to move his things back in the *haus,* and he has to stay with me until she leaves."

Rachel giggled. "You're blushing!"

"We have to sleep in the same room!" Hannah said in a high pitch.

"Isn't that what married couples are supposed to do?" Rachel asked, rolling her eyes.

Hannah sighed and jumped up from her chair, crossing to the window and looking out at Alana, who was coming toward the house.

"Under normal circumstances, that would be correct," she said hastily. "But you know he isn't ready to be a husband to me, and he might never be, but she threatened to go to the Bishop and have our marriage annulled. So now we have to make it look like we are a regular married couple so she'll leave us alone! She thinks she is better-suited to be Mira's *mamm* than me. Promise me you won't say anything to her!"

"Why would I tell her?" she said. "No one is better-suited to be her *mamm* than you. Besides, it's none of her business, but I hope you know what you're getting yourself into."

"Ach, me too!"

Alana let herself into the house and reached to take the baby from Rachel, but she stopped her with a look. "I'm not finished feeding her!"

Alana whipped her head around to Hannah. "Who is she holding onto my sister's baby? Is this your nanny?"

"Nee, I'm her *schweschder,* Mira's *aenti*—the same as you!" Rachel said boldly.

"No!" Alana said through gritted teeth. "You're not the same at all. I'm blood-related and should be raising her instead of your sister, who is involved in a marriage of lies."

"It isn't lies," Rachel snapped before Hannah could say a word. "Eli needed some time to heal from his loss."

"It's only been a few days!" Alana shot back. "That's all my sister meant to him? She doesn't even get a proper mourning period from her husband?"

"It seems to me that *you* intend to take that mourning period from him—that *you* should marry him instead. Should he be a proper husband to *you* if he marries you? Or should he *grow* to love his new *fraa?*"

"Seems to me he wasted no time—or maybe he's only trying to make me *think* he has so I'll be on my way. I'm not going anywhere!"

Hannah's heart did a somersault behind her ribcage. Would nothing make this woman leave them alone?

Just then, Eli came in with some wild, yellow daisies from the meadow and handed them to Hannah, kissing her lightly on the cheek. "I thought these might look nice on the table for dinner; I know how much you like wildflowers."

"Wouldn't those be better for my sister's grave?" Alana asked, her eyes narrowed on Eli. "I noticed there aren't any flowers at her grave-side, and that's shameful, given the so-called support she has from this community."

"I believe flowers are for the living," Eli said sternly. "Your *schweschder* was not shallow like that or selfish. She would be happy knowing I've brought flowers into the house to share with *mei familye.* She also liked having fresh-picked flowers in the *haus,* and I'm going to continue to bring them—to Hannah and Mira now."

Alana marched toward the door. "I *love* how every one of you has forgotten my sister so quickly."

"It seems to me that *you* forgot her while she was still alive, and now you want to come in here and convince us you loved her so much that you want to take over everything in her life now that she's gone? Where were you when she was here with us, missing you? You could have come back home and been a guest at our wedding, and a part of her life, and even been there when she took her last breath, but you weren't. Don't come into this *haus* and try to make anyone here believe you were a *gut schweschder.* The time for that was when she was still alive."

Eli hadn't meant to be so harsh, but she'd pushed her limits with him.

Alana rushed from the house and slammed the door behind her. Hannah, who was still standing at the sink, watched her run into the *dawdi haus* with her hand over her mouth.

She was crying, and Hannah felt compelled to go to her and comfort her.

Chapter 18

"She what?" Hannah asked loudly.

"She offered me a job at her advertisement agency answering the phone and filing papers," Rachel said excitedly. "She's going to teach me how to use the computer."

"Why would you want to be around Alana?" Hannah asked. "She's selfish and worldly."

She looked at her little sister with her day-dreamy eyes, and realized that was *exactly* Alana's appeal to her. She could offer her a life she'd been craving for far too long; she and her band of wild cousins that hang out in town constantly. If her *mamm* were still alive, she knew

Rachel wouldn't be so out of control. She'd tried her best to fill her *mamm's* shoes and take care of her sister, but she had a wild streak in her that just couldn't be tamed, no matter how much punishment their *daed* threatened her with.

The only good news in Rachel's statement was that it made it sound as if Alana was thinking of leaving.

She regretted letting Rachel go to comfort her instead of going herself, but she hadn't shown up for the evening meal, and with Mira being fussy, Hannah agreed to let her sister take a plate of food to her. She hadn't paid too much attention to the time, thinking the girl had come back in the house and was washing the dishes. But once she'd put Mira down to sleep, she came back downstairs to a messy kitchen, completely devoid of her sister.

Now, she ran some dishwater in the sink and watched the girl with a farther-off look in her eyes than usual, and asked her to help with a task that held no meaning to her. She didn't want to be Amish any more than Hannah wanted to be an *Englischer*.

"*Daed* will not let you go!"

Rachel shook her head. "He told me as long as I go with the cousins, I can go, and he agreed to help me with a little money to get an apartment. But now since I have a job waiting for me, he's sure to let me go."

Hannah sighed, knowing her *daed* didn't know what to do with Rachel any more than she did. Perhaps she'd been too caught up in her own whirlwind life to notice Rachel had grown away from her. She really thought that having her help with her new home and baby would help settle her down a bit, but it would seem it had only had the opposite effect on her. she knew there would be no stopping her if she had permission from their *daed,* and so supporting her decision would be the only thing that would keep communication open between them.

"Promise me you won't just run off without telling me goodbye," Hannah said.

Her expression fell. "I'm not even sure I'm going."

Hannah's ears perked up, though she feigned sympathy for her younger sister. "What do you mean?"

"She said several times *if* she returns. But she did say that if she doesn't, she has a friend who can take her business over and I can work for her!"

"Seems a little like an unstable promise to me," Hannah said as she sank her hands into the warm, sudsy dishwater, flinging some bubbles at

Rachel with a giggle. "Alana is just a little too wishy-washy, so promise me you won't come back here being like that."

Handing a dry towel to her sister, she turned and noticed Alana behind her. She hadn't heard the kitchen door, and wondered just how long Alana had been standing there holding her dirty dishes in her hands.

Chapter 19

Hannah rolled over to a gurgling baby beside her, and wondered how she'd gotten there. She panicked thinking she could have gotten up and put the infant in bed with her without so much as waking up. Was she really that exhausted?

When the bedroom door opened, she turned and saw Eli enter the room with a bottle for the baby. He must have put Mira in bed with her, but had she been sleeping so soundly that she hadn't heard her cry? Then she remembered finding Eli asleep in the oversized chair beside the bed, with his feet propped up on the ottoman. She'd draped a quilt over him before getting into bed. Though she was grateful he was sleeping in the chair, she felt guilty for taking the bed when he surely had to be uncomfortable sleeping there.

She sat up and held her hand out for the bottle, but he set it down on the bedside table between the bed and the chair, then lifted his daughter from beside Hannah and sat down in the chair with her. He tucked a burp-cloth under her chin and held the bottle for her, smiling at her.

"I'm your *daed,"* he said softly. "I'm going to help take care of you, and I'm going to protect you and teach you what you need to know to grow up and be just as special as *both* your *mamms."*

Hannah could hear the shakiness of his voice, and it brought tears to her eyes that he would include her as Mira's mother. She watched him in the pale moonlight that filtered in through the sheer curtains on the windows. He was truly a handsome and loving man, and she was lucky to have him.

If it was possible, she fell even more in love with him right then and there as she continued to watch him care for his infant daughter. It was an answer to many prayers, but she still had one unanswered—that Eli would someday be able to return that love to her.

He held Mira up on his shoulder to burp her.

"How am I doing?" he asked. "I've watched you, and it seems this is what you do."

She giggled lightly. "You're doing everything right. You're going to be a *gut daed* to her."

"*Danki,*" he said. "I don't know what I was so afraid of. Loving her, I suppose. I think I was so afraid of losing her that I didn't want to get too close to her."

"That's understandable," Hannah said, propping herself up on her elbow to face him. "After *mei mamm* died, I would go to visit your *mamm* and cook with her because I needed a *mamm* so badly that I convinced myself she was the perfect replacement. But after a while, I stopped going because I was afraid she would leave me too. I suppose that helps me to be a little sympathetic for Alana."

"I suppose we should keep her in our prayers," he said as he rocked Mira.

Hannah flopped back down on her pillow and yawned, which caused Eli to yawn.

"How long before she's going to wake back up again wanting another bottle?" he asked.

She giggled. "In a couple of hours!"

"Then I better get her back in the cradle and get to sleep myself," he said. "This farm wakes up at the same time every morning no matter how much sleep I get."

She giggled softly in agreement as she watched him place the sleeping baby gently back in her cradle.

He went to the chair and picked up the quilt, and then pivoted toward the bed where Hannah was.

Without a word, she pulled open the covers on that side of the bed inviting him in.

He slipped in the bed facing her and reached up to push back a stray hair from her face. His touch sent a fluttering desire through her, but she suppressed it.

He surprised her by pulling her close and kissing her full on the mouth. She deepened the kiss, but only for a moment, not wanting things to go too far too fast. He kissed her forehead and tucked her under his arm with her head resting on his shoulder. She was content to cuddle with him while she listened to his soft breath in the quiet night that mixed with the equally-beautiful sound of Mira's.

Chapter 20

Hannah bolted upright in a half-sleep state when she first heard the creaking of the floorboards. Forcing her eyes open; she first glanced at the sleeping baby in the cradle, as she felt the empty spot next to her in the bed. Daylight had not quite reached the room, but it was enough to see that it was Eli, fully-dressed, toting *two* cups of coffee, who was in the room.

She flopped back down to the mattress, relieved that her instincts were wrong for a change, and there was no reason for her to get up.

Eli sat on the edge of the bed and handed her a cup of coffee with cream—surprisingly, just the way she liked it. She took a sip, wondering if he expected her to help him with chores in the mornings. She wasn't opposed to helping with gathering the eggs and milking Greta, but she was certainly used to doing much more.

"Did I oversleep?" she asked, taking a sip of the coffee. She could get used to him bringing her coffee.

He climbed in next to her, his shoes already off, and she assumed he left them in the mudroom. She sat up next to him and he opened his arm to her, pulling her close enough to rest her head on his shoulder. This was something she could get used to.

"I was wondering if you'd like to take a sleigh ride with me later."

"A sleigh ride?" she asked jumping from the bed and peering out the window at the thick blanket of snow that had fallen overnight.

She looked back at him. "There must be at least three inches of snow!" she whispered.

"It's more like four," he said. "I had to shovel the walkway for you."

"*Danki.*"

"Will you ask Rachel to watch Mira for about an hour so I can take you for that sleigh ride?"

"Do you think that's a *gut* idea to leave her here alone with Mira when Alana is lurking around?"

"She's gone!" he said, pulling an envelope from his shirt pocket with a smile. "She left a note. Read it for yourself."

Daylight was beginning to seep into the room, and it was just enough light to read the note by. She ran through it quickly, getting to the part where Alana said it was best if she left.

"This is wonderful news," she said loudly, and then hushed herself.

Mira stretched and yawned, causing her parents to smile at one another.

"So what do you say?" he asked. "Will you do me the honor of allowing me to court you properly by going for a sleigh ride with me later?"

"Courting?" she asked. "Are you sure?"

He kissed her lightly on her cheek and then smiled over at Mira and nodded.

"*Jah,* I'm sure!"

THE END

Look for Rachel's Secret: Book Three in this series.

You might also enjoy:

Little Wild Flower: Book One

Hippie-Chick meets Amish guy next door! Jane Abigail Reeves is Little Wild Flower. Raised in the city; Jane and her family move to a farmhouse in a rural Amish community in Indiana as a respite for her alcoholic mother. When she stumbles upon her handsome Amish neighbor, Elijah, she sets out to teach him her big city ways, while he introduces her to the quiet life of the Amish.

Attempting to convert him to her hippie lifestyle, she finds herself drawn to his ways, unable to deny her love for him.
Set in the 1970's, Jane's story is full of cultural obstacles she must overcome in order to put an end to the dysfunction of her family's past.
Can a hippie-chick like Jane find friendship and more with an Amish man, despite their cultural differences?

Little Wild Flower: Book 2

Just when Jane thought her life in the Amish community couldn't get any better, tragedy strikes the Zook farm. Jane suddenly feels lost in the world she created with Elijah, and flees to her home town in search of her childhood friends. Will coming face-to-face with the pain of her childhood send her running back to the farm, or will she cling to the life she left behind as a teenaged girl?

Little Wild Flower: Book 3

BOOK 3: Little Wild Flower series
When tragedy strikes her brother's family, Jane struggles to find a way to make peace with it all, while managing the growing pains taking place within her own family unit.

When the new doctor turns out to be none other than Bradley, Jane's childhood sweetheart, she struggles with his new affections, feeling as though she is betraying the memory of her life with Elijah, her deceased husband; the very life that caused her to blend with the Amish community. As she comes to terms with her life without Elijah, she quickly begins to reject some of the Amish traditions, yet keeps others. When she slowly lets go of the life she lost, she discovers that starting over doesn't have to be as difficult as she feared.

Little Wild Flower: Book 4

Amish Wildflowers continuing story...
All Jane wants is to be a normal child, but she's convinced she needs super-powers to help her survive her tormented childhood at the hands of her alcoholic mother.
By the time she reaches her teen years, Jane is tired of living in fear, feeling she is about to break. When a friend tells her that he believes it's her destiny to save her mother's life--the very person who'd been so cruel to

her, when the opportunity presents itself, Jane doesn't believe she's up to the challenge, since she wishes only the opposite for her mother.
Will she be brave enough to look beyond her own pain and find the strength to save them both, or will Jane become a sacrificial lamb for her mother's sake?

This book contains some mildly disturbing situations in order to maintain the authenticity of the story of Jane's stormy childhood with her alcoholic mother—before she found Jesus and got saved.
Jane's story is based on true events…

Check out these other titles too!

Please LIKE my Facebook Page HERE

Made in the USA
Lexington, KY
03 December 2016